Katie and the Mona Lisa

James Mayhew

ORCHARD BOOKS / NEW YORK

For my wife,
Maria Antonietta De Salve,
who has a lovely smile

To find out more about the *Mona Lisa* and Italian Renaissance painters,
turn to the end of the book.

Orchard Books, A Grolier Company, 95 Madison Avenue, New York, NY 10016

Manufactured in Belgium. Book design by Mina Greenstein
The text of this book is set in 16 point Galliard. The illustrations are watercolor.
3 5 7 9 10 8 6 4 2

Library of Congress Cataloging-in-Publication Data
Mayhew, James, date.
Katie and the Mona Lisa / James Mayhew.—1st American ed.   p.   cm.
Summary: At the art museum, while her grandmother dozes, Katie steps into the painting of the Mona Lisa, and together they have
adventures with the characters from four other well-known Renaissance paintings. Includes information about the artists.
ISBN 0-531-30177-X (trade : alk. paper)
1. Leonardo da Vinci, 1452–1519. Mona Lisa—Juvenile fiction.
[1. Leonardo da Vinci, 1452–1519. Mona Lisa—Fiction. 2. Art museums—Fiction. 3. Museums—Fiction. 4. Art, Italian—Fiction.
5. Art, Renaissance—Italy—Fiction. 6. Artists—Fiction.]
I. Title. PZ7.M4684Karf 1999 [E]—dc21 98-41162

$\mathcal{K}$atie and her grandma often went to the museum on their days out together. Grandma liked to tell Katie all about the famous paintings.

"Which picture do you like best?" asked Grandma.

"Mona Lisa," said Katie. "She smiled at me."

"She smiles at everyone," said Grandma. "That's why she's famous."

"What makes her smile?" asked Katie.

"I don't know," said Grandma, resting on a chair. "Perhaps you should have a closer look at her."

"'*Mona Lisa* by Leonardo da Vinci,'" said Katie, reading the note by the painting. "I wish I knew what is making you smile."

"Then come inside, *bambina!*" said Mona Lisa.

Katie was very surprised. But Grandma was dozing and the museum was empty. So Katie climbed over the frame and inside the picture.

Mona Lisa was sitting in a grand room with a balcony.

"*Bambina!*" she said. "How lovely to see you. I have not had a visitor for hundreds of years!"

"That's a long time," said Katie. "Don't you get lonely?"

"Yes, very," said Mona Lisa. "I am supposed to smile, but I don't feel very happy at all."

Mona Lisa started to look sad. A small tear ran down her cheek, and her smile disappeared.

"I'll cheer you up," said Katie, handing her a handkerchief.

"When Leonardo painted me, he asked clowns and musicians to make me smile," said Mona Lisa, blowing her nose.

"Can you dance or sing?"

"Yes, but I've got a better idea," said Katie. She took Mona Lisa by the hand, and very carefully they stepped out of the painting and into the museum.

"You can meet anyone you like here," said Katie. "I'm sure there is someone who can make you smile again."

They looked at the paintings, one by one.

At last they stopped in front of *St. George and the Dragon* by Raphael.

"A knight in shining armor!" said Mona Lisa. "Can I meet him?"

"If we climb inside," said Katie.

So Mona Lisa gathered up her long skirts, and Katie took her through the frame.

St. George was rescuing a beautiful princess from a
fire-breathing dragon. But he forgot all about her
when he saw Mona Lisa.

"Ah! *Bella!*" he said, climbing off his horse. He
kissed Mona Lisa gallantly on the hand.

At once the dragon ran off and started to chase the princess again.

"Mamma mia!" said Mona Lisa.

"Help! Save me!" cried the princess. She leaped out of the picture, with the dragon flying after her.

St. George grabbed his lance and dashed off to the rescue.

"Now I'm all alone again," sighed
Mona Lisa.

"Perhaps we can try another painting,"
suggested Katie.

They climbed out of the painting and
walked into another room.

Mona Lisa pointed to a painting by Sandro Botticelli, called
Primavera, which means spring.

"Look at the dancers!" she said. "I'd love to meet them!"

So Katie clambered inside, and Mona Lisa quickly followed her.

Katie and Mona Lisa found themselves in an enchanted grove where everyone was dancing. The sweet scent of flowers filled the air.

"Welcome to springtime," said a beautiful woman in a flowery dress.
"I am Flora. Come with me and taste the oranges."

Flora helped Katie gather sweet, juicy oranges from the
trees, while Mona Lisa joined in the dance.
"I think I could be happy if I stayed here," she said.

But Katie slipped and fell on top of the three dancers. They all ended up on the ground, covered with squashed oranges.

"You have ruined the springtime dance!" They started to chase Katie.

"Perhaps it's best if we don't stay," said Katie.

"I think you may be right," sighed Mona Lisa.

They quickly climbed out of the painting and ran into another room before the three dancers could catch them.

Mona Lisa saw a painting called *The Lion of St. Mark* by Vittore Carpaccio.

She recognized the city of Venice behind the lion. "I've always wanted to visit Venice," sighed Mona Lisa.

Katie thought it would be a good place to hide from the angry dancers. She took Mona Lisa's hand, and they went through the frame and into the painting.

The lion was very friendly. "Welcome to Venice!" he said.

"There's water everywhere," said Katie. "Is there a flood?"

"Venice was built on the sea," said the lion. "I shall carry you over the water."

They climbed onto the lion's back, and he opened his beautiful rainbow wings and flew up into the sky.

Below them Venice sparkled like silver and gold.

The lion carried them to the Grand Canal, and
they jumped into a boat called a gondola.

The people of Venice waved, sang songs, and gave
them pasta and ice cream to eat. Katie wanted to
have seconds of everything, but just then she noticed
that the gondola had sprung a leak.

"My dress will be ruined!" cried Mona Lisa. "What shall we do?"

"I'll fly you back to the picture frame," said the lion. "Climb on!"

They held on to the lion's mane, and he flew up into the sky.

"I'm slipping off!" yelled Katie, hanging on to one of the lion's wings.

"Oh dear," said the lion, "I think I'm going to . . . *crash!*"

They flew straight through the frame and tumbled into the museum.

"*Mamma mia!*" said Mona Lisa.

There, in front of them, sat the dragon. He puffed out clouds of smoke and roared at them.

And behind the dragon stood St. George and the princess, and the three dancers. They all looked very angry.

"Oh dear, what a muddle!" said Katie. "What shall we do?"

Suddenly the museum was filled with sweet music. It was coming from another picture, *An Angel with a Lute*, painted by a student of Leonardo da Vinci.

The angel stepped out of his painting and stroked the dragon. He stopped growling, lay down, and wagged his tail.

"How clever!" said the princess. "You've tamed him!"

The princess put her belt around his neck and led him proudly back to the painting.

St. George kissed Mona Lisa's hand once more and followed them.

The angel played on, and the three dancers gracefully smiled
and twirled and skipped happily back to the orange grove.
The lion flew back to Venice, roaring a farewell.

"Please, can you help Mona Lisa?" said Katie to the angel. "I wanted to make her smile, but everything went wrong."

"She doesn't need my help," said the angel. "Just look!"

And Katie saw that Mona Lisa *was* smiling.

"Mamma mia!" she said. "What an adventure we've had, *bambina.* Wasn't it fun?"

"Yes, it was," said Katie, and they both laughed.

Katie thanked the angel and watched him fly back into his painting.

"Will you be happy in your painting?" Katie said to Mona Lisa.

"I shall think of you and that will make me laugh," she said, climbing through the frame. "Thank you for making me smile again, *bambina. Addio.*"

"*Addio!*" said Katie.

Katie ran back to her grandma.

"I found out all about Mona Lisa's smile!" said Katie. "But I can't tell you, because you wouldn't believe me."

"You're probably right," said Grandma. "Now what would you like for supper?"

"Pasta and ice cream," said Katie. "They're my favorite."
And she smiled a secret smile, just like Mona Lisa.

Mona Lisa *and the Italian Renaissance*

The paintings in this book were painted during the Renaissance, which means "rebirth" or "new beginning." The Renaissance was a time of great change in which painters, writers, and musicians created wonderful works of art, and scientists, inventors, and explorers discovered new and amazing things. The Renaissance started in Italy, and that is where the paintings in this book come from.

LEONARDO DA VINCI (1452–1519)

Leonardo was an inventor, scientist, mathematician, and explorer, as well as an artist. The *Mona Lisa* was one of Leonardo's favorite paintings. Her smile is supposed to be very mysterious. Some people say that Mona Lisa was entertained by clowns and jugglers while she posed for the painting, and that is what made her smile. The *Mona Lisa* can be seen in the Louvre museum in Paris, France. The picture of the angel was painted by one of Leonardo's students. It is called *An Angel with a Lute* and can be seen at the National Gallery in London, England.

SANDRO BOTTICELLI (1445–1510)

Botticelli's real name was Alessandro di Mariano Filipepi, and he probably took the name Botticelli from the Italian word meaning "beater of gold," because when he was a young man, he worked with a goldsmith. Botticelli painted many large wall paintings called frescoes, as well as pictures like the *Primavera*. You can see the *Primavera* in the Uffizi Gallery in Florence, Italy.

RAPHAEL (1483–1520)

Raphael's real name was Raffaello Sanzio. He studied art with Leonardo and other great painters. Raphael liked to paint scenes from dramatic stories, many of which came from legends and from the Bible. You can see his painting of *St. George and the Dragon* at the National Gallery of Art in Washington, D.C.

VITTORE CARPACCIO (1460–1525/6)

Carpaccio told stories through his paintings. He is best known for his paintings showing different scenes from one story. Carpaccio lived in Venice; the winged lion in his painting is the symbolic protector of Venice. This painting is still in the Duke's Palace in Venice, Italy.

You will find many other wonderful paintings and drawings by these and other Renaissance artists in museums all over the world.

ACKNOWLEDGMENTS

Mona Lisa by Leonardo da Vinci; Musée d'Louvre; © Photo RMN—R.G. Ojeda. *An Angel with a Lute* by Associate of Leonardo; Reproduced by courtesy of the trustees of the National Gallery, London. *St. George and the Dragon* by Raphael; © Board of Trustees, National Gallery of Art, Washington, D.C. BEN558. *Primavera,* c. 1478 (tempera on panel) by Sandro Botticelli (1445–1510); Galleria degli Uffizi, Italy/Bridgeman Art Library, London FTB60402. *The Lion of St. Mark* by Vittore Carpaccio (c. 1460–1525); Palazzo Ducale, Venice/Bridgeman Art Library, London.